The Monster Story-Teller

By Jacqueline Wilson
Illustrated by Nick Sharratt

CORGI PUPS

www.booksattransworld.co.uk/childrens

For Sean William MacLachlan

Also available by Jacqueline Wilson
and published by Doubleday/Corgi Pups:
THE DINOSAUR'S PACKED LUNCH

Published by Young Corgi Books:
LIZZIE ZIPMOUTH

Published by Doubleday/Corgi Yearling:
BAD GIRLS
THE BED AND BREAKFAST STAR
BURIED ALIVE!
CLIFFHANGER
THE DARE GAME
DOUBLE ACT
GLUBBSLYME
THE LOTTIE PROJECT
THE MUM-MINDER
THE STORY OF TRACY BEAKER
THE SUITCASE KID
THE ILLUSTRATED MUM
VICKY ANGEL

THE MONSTER STORY-TELLER
A CORGI PUPS BOOK : 0 552 545295

First published in Great Britain by Doubleday,
a division of Transworld Publishers

PRINTING HISTORY
Doubleday edition published 1997
Corgi Pups edition published 1997

7 9 10 8

Copyright © 1997 by Jacqueline Wilson
Illustrations copyright © 1997 by Nick Sharratt

The right of Jacqueline Wilson to be identified as the author of this work has been
asserted in accordance with the Copyright, Designs and Patents Act 1988

Set in 19/23pt Bembo Infant.

Corgi Pups Books are published by Transworld Publishers,
61–63 Uxbridge Road, London W5 5SA,
a division of The Random House Group Ltd,
in Australia by Random House Australia (Pty) Ltd,
20 Alfred Street, Milsons Point, Sydney, NSW 2061, Australia,
and in New Zealand by Random House New Zealand Ltd,
18 Poland Road, Glenfield, Auckland 10, New Zealand
and in South Africa by Random House (Pty) Ltd,
Endulini, 5a Jubilee Road, Parktown 2193, South Africa.

Printed and bound in Great Britain by
Cox & Wyman Ltd, Reading, Berkshire.

CONTENTS

Series Reading Consultant: Prue Goodwin,
Reading and Language Information Centre,
University of Reading.

Chapter One

Natalie was fed up.

The class were doing a project on flying.

She had made a big bird but his wings went wonky. He wouldn't fly.

Natalie talked to her friends.

"What did you do on Saturday?" Natalie asked.

"I went swimming," said Clare.

"I went to McDonald's," said Zoe.

"I went to the football match," said Lee.

"I went shopping with my nan," said Clive. "She gave me five pounds. And she bought me chocolates. Yum yum."

"Do you want to hear what I did on Saturday?" said Natalie. "First I went swimming and there were real dolphins in the pool and they gave me a ride. Then I went to McDonald's and I had twenty Big Macs and twenty strawberry milk shakes. And then

I went to this football match and I was the mascot and I scored a goal and everyone cheered. And then I went shopping with my nan and she gave me fifty pounds and lots and lots and lots of chocolates."

"How many chocolates?" said Clive.

"Natalie's telling stories, silly,"
said Lee.

"Settle down, children!" said
Mr Hunter. "Natalie, get on with
your work and stop telling stories.
It's not story-time until this
afternoon — when we're going to
have a special treat."

"I want a special treat now,"
Natalie muttered. "This is boring,
boring, boring."

She sighed.

She stretched.

She looked up at the window.
She looked at the plant in the pot
on the window sill.

And the plant in the pot moved.

Natalie blinked.

The plant in the pot moved again. Upwards!

Was the plant in the pot flying? Then Natalie saw!

The plant in the pot wasn't flying.

It was the saucer.

It was an ordinary flower-patterned saucer. But today it had grown wings.

"Of course!" said Natalie. "It's a flying saucer!"

She went to have a closer look.

There was a little creature standing in the saucer.

Was it an ant?

"A flying ant!" Natalie giggled.

It wasn't an ant.

It was a very, very, very tiny monster.

It had wild hair and pointy teeth and sharp claws and a long tail.

But it didn't look fierce. It looked friendly.

"Hello!" said Natalie.

"Hello!" said the tiny monster.

"Can you speak up a bit?" said Natalie. "I can't hear you properly."

"I'm shouting!" said the tiny monster. "Can you speak down a bit? You're hurting my ears."

"Is it your flying saucer?"
Natalie whispered, so softly her
lips scarcely moved.

The tiny monster nodded
proudly.

"Want to see me do twirlie-
whirlies?" he said.

"You bet!" said Natalie.

The tiny monster tapped his teeny foot.

The saucer flapped its little wings and whizzed round and round in the air. The plant's leaves waved wildly.

The tiny monster waved too as he circled Natalie's head, round and round until she got dizzy.

The plant wobbled and wobbled until...

...it tipped right off the saucer and
crashed onto the classroom floor!

"Oh help!" said the tiny
monster.

"Oh help!" said Natalie.
"What's Mr Hunter going to say?"

Chapter Two

Mr Hunter said plenty.
"You naughty girl, Natalie!

What were you doing over by the
window? Did you knock that
plant over on purpose?"

"No! It wasn't me," said
Natalie.

"It was me!" said the tiny
monster, flying his saucer behind
Natalie.

"Look at the mess on the floor! Go and fetch a dustpan and brush from the store cupboard, Natalie," said Mr Hunter. "And take that silly smile off your face. It isn't funny."

Natalie couldn't help smiling. The tiny monster was tickling the back of her neck with his weeny claws.

Natalie hurried out of the classroom.

The flying saucer went with her, whirling round her head.

"Where are you going?" shouted the tiny monster.

"To fetch the dustpan and brush," said Natalie.

"Boring, boring, boring," said the tiny monster. "Come flying with me instead. Jump up on my saucer."

"I can't," said Natalie. "I'm much too big. I'd smash the saucer. And squash you."

"I can make you small," said the tiny monster. "Hold my hand."

Natalie held out her great big hand. The tiny monster held out his weeny little paw.

Then Natalie started shrinking!

She felt as if she were being rubbed with very powerful magic soap.

She got smaller and smaller and smaller until she was exactly the same size as the tiny monster. Only he didn't look tiny now.

The monster's hair was very
wild.

His teeth were very pointy.

His claws were very sharp.

His tail was very long.

But he still didn't look fierce.

He looked friendly.

"Let's fly," said the monster.
"Shall we go fast?"

"You bet!" said Natalie.

The monster tapped his paw
and the wings flapped very fast
indeed. The flying saucer whizzed
way down the school corridor.

"Aaaaah!" said Natalie.

"This is easy-peasy slowcoach stuff," said the monster, showing off like mad. "Let's go outside."

Natalie nodded.

She didn't have any breath left for talking.

They flew very fast across the playground.

"Wheeeeee!" said Natalie. "This is wonderful! Can we go right over the rooftops?"

"You bet!" said the monster.

They did twirlie-whirlies round
the chimney-pots.

"Now let's do swoopie-doopies," said the monster.

They swooped right down to the park.

The duck pond looked like a puddle from high in the sky, but when they got nearer and nearer...

...the ducks started to get bigger and bigger.

"Quick! Fly up or they'll get us!" said Natalie.

"Chicken," teased the monster.

"No – duck!" said Natalie.

They swooped up just in time, leaving the ducks quacking foolishly.

"I live near the park," said
Natalie. "There's my house.
Look, there's my mum and my
little brothers!"

"Hey, do you want to see my
mum and my little brothers?" said
the monster.

"You bet!" said Natalie.

"OK. Monster Planet, here we come!"

Chapter Three

The flying saucer's wings grew immensely.

They flapped faster and faster and faster.

The flying saucer shot straight into the sky. It flew higher than the tallest buildings in the whole world...

...higher than the world itself, away to a different planet altogether.

Monster Planet.

"There it is!" shouted the monster.

"It's little!" said Natalie.

"So are we," said the monster.

"I can see water," said Natalie.

"It's our seaside," said the monster.

"I can see lots of little monster people!" said Natalie.

They had wild hair and pointy teeth and sharp claws and long tails. But they didn't look fierce. They looked friendly.

"Shall we go for a sail?" said the monster.

"You bet!" said Natalie. "Hey, do you have dolphins?"

"Watch!" said the monster, and he whistled.

Six special monster dolphins
leapt out of the water and
whistled back.
The smiliest special monster
dolphin gave Natalie a ride.

"That was wonderful," said
Natalie. "But I'm all wet now."

"We have special drying
dragons on the beach," said the
monster, parking the flying
saucer.

"Do you want the warm
dragon, the hot dragon, or the
special sauna dragon?" said the
monster.

"Just the warm one, please,"
said Natalie.

She was wonderfully warm in
seconds.

The monster had the special
sauna treatment and was so red-
hot he fried an egg on himself
and ate it!

"Do you want an egg too, Natalie?" said the monster.

"Maybe not an egg," said Natalie. "But I am starving."

"Do you want to go to McMonsters?" said the monster.

"You bet!" said Natalie.

Natalie ate a McMonster
burger. And another and another
and another.

Whenever she got thirsty she
went to the pretty pink fountain.
It was strawberry monster milk
shake!

"I think I'm full up now," said
Natalie.

"Let's go and look round the
shops," said the monster.

"I haven't got any money,"
said Natalie.

"No problem," said the
monster. "Monster money grows
on trees, look. Just help yourself!"

So Natalie and the monster picked a pocketful of monster money and went to the monster shopping centre.

There was a monster pet shop with monster dogs and monster cats and monster rabbits and monster hamsters and monster mice.

Natalie liked the monster birds best. She bought them all so she could let them out of their cages.

The monster birds flapped their wings and flew far away.

"Let's go in the sports shop," said the monster.

"Yes! I'll buy that football," said Natalie.

"Who do you support?" said the monster. "I like the Monster Marvels."

"Me too," said Natalie.

"Do you want to go to the match?" said the monster.

"You bet!" said Natalie.

The monster football stadium
was packed out.

Natalie and the monster got
specially shown to their seats.

"Up the Monster Marvels!"
yelled Natalie.

They all waved to her when
they ran onto the pitch.

"Come and kick off for us,
Natalie," they shouted.

Natalie scored a stupendous goal.

"Hurray for Natalie!" shouted all the monsters, while she leapt in the air.

The monster took Natalie to meet his monster nan after the match.

Monster Nan made a great fuss of them both. She gave them hot chocolate to drink and cold chocolate ice-cream to eat – and lots and lots and lots of chocolate bars.

"Don't tell your mum or she'll fuss about your teeth," said Monster Nan.

"I want to see your mum and your little brothers," said Natalie.

"Right," said the monster. "Hop back on the flying saucer."

They flew over the monster's house.

"There they are! That's my monster mum. And my little monster brothers."

"My brothers are little monsters too!" said Natalie.

"Why aren't you at school, you bad little monster?" shouted his monster mum.

"Uh oh. School!" said the monster.

"Off you go!" said Monster Mum.

They flew to Monster School. The monster teacher had wild hair and pointy teeth and sharp claws and a long tail.

He looked very fierce.

He didn't look friendly.

"Where on earth have you been? And who is this strange girl?" said the monster teacher.

"She's my friend Natalie from another planet. We've whizzed back here from Earth," said the monster.

"You're telling stories again!" said the monster teacher. "You're in big trouble, little monster."

"Oh help!" said the monster. "Let's go, Natalie!"

They jumped back on the saucer.

"Planet Earth, ever so quickly, please!" said the monster.

The saucer flew down and down and down, all the way back to Earth...

...right above Natalie's school.

"I don't think I want to go back," said Natalie. "I think I might be in big trouble too. I'd sooner stay with you and have MONSTER FUN."

Chapter Four

"I don't want to say goodbye!" said Natalie.

"Don't worry. I'll come back," said the monster.

"Promise?" said Natalie.

"You bet!" said the monster.

Natalie got ready to jump off the saucer. Then she saw a HUGE monster.

"Aaaaah!" said Natalie.

"Miaow," said the huge monster.

"It's the school cat!" said Natalie. "But it's much bigger than me now."

"Shake my hand, silly," said the monster. "Then you'll grow big again."

Natalie clasped the monster's paw and immediately started growing again.

"Get off my saucer before I get squashed!" said the tiny monster.

Natalie jumped to the ground as she grew to her proper size.

She waved goodbye, stroked the cat, grabbed the dustpan and brush, and ran back to her classroom.

"Natalie!" shouted Mr Hunter. "Where on earth have you been?"

"I haven't been anywhere on Earth, Mr Hunter. Wait till I tell you," said Natalie.

She told everyone her story about Monster Planet. Everyone loved Natalie's story. Everyone but Mr Hunter.

"You're telling stories again, Natalie!"

Guess what. Natalie was in big trouble.

Natalie cheered up that afternoon. A special visitor came to the school. A story-teller.

She told the children stories about mice and clowns and princes and elephants and gingerbread men.

"And now I'll tell you my favourite story," said the story-teller. "It's all about monsters!"

"Once upon a time there was this very, very, very tiny monster with wild hair and pointy teeth and sharp claws and a long tail. This tiny monster had his very own flying saucer," said the story-teller.

"That's Natalie's story!" said all the children. "Natalie's told us that story already, Miss."

"Come out here, Natalie. So you like telling stories?" said the story-teller.

"You bet!" said Natalie.

"Maybe you'll be a story-teller like me when you grow up."

"Do you want to tell the Monster Story, Natalie?" said the story-teller.

"Well, it is my story," said Natalie.

"It's my story too," said a teeny tiny voice.

So they all told the Monster Story together.

THE END